# MOONBEAM'S
## ARCTIC ADVENTURE

**FOOTPRINTS for the FUTURE**

*The Flying Squirrel*

**Picture Stories for Young Readers**

First impression: 2018
© Molly Janet Holborn, David Morgan Williams & Y Lolfa Cyf., 2018

Cover picture / illustration: Maria Moss

ISBN: 978 1 78461 618 2

Published and printed in Wales
on paper from well-maintained forests by
Y Lolfa Cyf., Talybont, Ceredigion SY24 5HE
*e-mail* ylolfa@ylolfa.com
*website* www.ylolfa.com
*tel* 01970 832 304
*fax* 832 782

# MOONBEAM'S
## ARCTIC ADVENTURE

WRITTEN BY MOLLY JANET HOLBORN
AND DAVID MORGAN WILLIAMS

ILLUSTRATED BY MARIA MOSS

yLolfa

To our beloved Jan, wife and grandmother, who passed away in April 2016. Every day her memory continues to inspire us.

To my Gramps, to write a children's book with you has brought me endless joy, for we are a team.

We want to say a huge thank you to our illustrator,
Maria Moss. Her outstanding artwork has visually brought
our characters to life. To aid in providing inspiration
for children's imaginations is an inspiring thing.

Secondly, we want to thank Laura Jenkins.
She was a crucial help in structuring our book in a way
that was perfect for our readers and we are truly grateful.

To everyone at Y Lolfa, their support and guidance
through the publication process was exceptional,
diolch yn fawr for bringing our book to life!

Once upon a time in Cardigan Bay, west Wales, there lived two mischievous bottlenose dolphins, one was called Moonbeam and the other Sunbeam.

They were the best of friends and they would swim together all the time, jumping and diving into the deep blue sea.

One sunny afternoon, Moonbeam and Sunbeam were playing a game of tag, when all of a sudden Moonbeam heard something. It was a distress signal.

"SUNBEAM! Something's wrong,

 I'm picking up a distress signal!" cried Moonbeam.

"Me too! Where do you think it's coming from?" asked Sunbeam.

"Sounds like up North to me," said Moonbeam.

Moonbeam stared out into the open sea trying to figure out their next move. He looked at Sunbeam for encouragement.

"Moonbeam, don't panic, we will find a way. We just have to put our heads together!" said Sunbeam.

"Right, well, since the signals are coming from the North we should swim in that direction," replied Moonbeam.

"Great idea, let's go!"

They swam as quickly as their bodies could carry them through the water, gliding over the waves like speedboats.

They were just about to rest when out of the blue came a giant tail flopping out of the ocean surface.

Moonbeam nudged Sunbeam in astonishment.

"What the kelp is that?" whispered Sunbeam.

"I have no idea, could it be some kind of Arctic fish?" replied Moonbeam.

"Well if it is, that's the weirdest looking fish in the entire ocean!"

Sunbeam swam closer to observe the strange thing moving ever so slowly and, when it began to rise, something else rose with it and a head popped up.

Smiling straight at him was a giant fin whale.

Sunbeam grinned at the large head that stood before him.

"Hey, what are you staring at?" asked the furious fin whale.

"Well, I think you have quite a funny face," replied Sunbeam.

"Oh hush up, long nose!"

"Stop teasing one another, you two!"
said Moonbeam, slowly coming towards them.

"Sorry," they replied in unison.

"I have something important to tell you," said the fin whale.

"I have been sending out distress signals as many humans and animals are in danger.

THE... THE... THE GREENLAND ICE CAP IS BREAKING UP AND LARGE ICEBERGS ARE FLOATING SOUTH!

It's v... v... e... e... rrr... y s... s... scary," spluttered the frightened whale.

"We picked up your distress signals," said Moonbeam, "that's why we're here. But please have courage, if we all work together we can do something to help."

"Oh, thank you so much," replied the whale. "I thought I might have to deal with this on my own, and… well… it's such a big problem, as you'll soon find out. If it's all right with you, I'll return to my family to ensure they're safe, but please, if you continue north, could you keep in touch bysending me messages.

I'll gladly come and help if you need me!"

Moonbeam suddenly realised what they must do.

He thanked the fin whale for his advice and he and Sunbeam swam north into the colder waters of the Arctic Ocean.

To pass the time, they did flips in the water as they glided through the waves.

Suddenly, Moonbeam saw something out of the corner of his eye, flying high above them.

Two beautiful Arctic terns gently landed themselves in front of the dolphins. Moonbeam kept staring at their wonderfully bright red beaks and their long, white, arched tails.

"Hello, I'm Tilley and this is my friend Terry. We have been watching your journey north and have come to tell you that what the fin whale said was true," gasped the tern, who was almost out of breath.

Moonbeam and Sunbeam discussed with the terns
how they were going to solve this icy problem.

"I've got it!" I know a starfish called Grace.
She's so sweet and I know she can help.
She can send pulses to the nearby shark clan.
Don't look so worried, they're not as bad as they sound,"
said Tilley, who was very proud of her brilliant idea.

It seemed like their only option. The terns gave clear directions
on how to find Grace's secret hideout, and the two dolphins
headed down to the seabed where they found large
numbers of beautiful sea anemones.

"I think we are lost"
said Sunbeam.

"We can't be, the terns
said it was right here!"
replied Moonbeam.

He was getting frustrated when,
suddenly, they heard something.

"Psst! Are you looking for Grace?"
chorused the sea anemones as they
swayed back and forth in the gentle current.

Moonbeam looked down and nudged Sunbeam.
The seabed looked like a floating carpet of flowers,
swaying in the ocean currents trying to catch lunch.

"Yes, we are looking for Grace, can you help us?"
asked Sunbeam.

"Of course, we are the guardians of her hideout, she doesn't
like the nasty old crabs which are always disturbing her,"
sang the sea anemones.

The anemones lifted their tickling tentacles
to uncover a cave only big enough for
one dolphin to enter.

Moonbeam volunteered to go in,
while Sunbeam waited nervously outside.

Moonbeam entered the cave cautiously.

He looked around and saw an orange-coloured starfish
on the ceiling of the cave. She jumped off and stared
mysteriously at Moonbeam.

"And you are?" asked Grace.

"I am Moonbeam and I really need your help!"

"Oh, and what do you want me to do?" grumbled Grace.

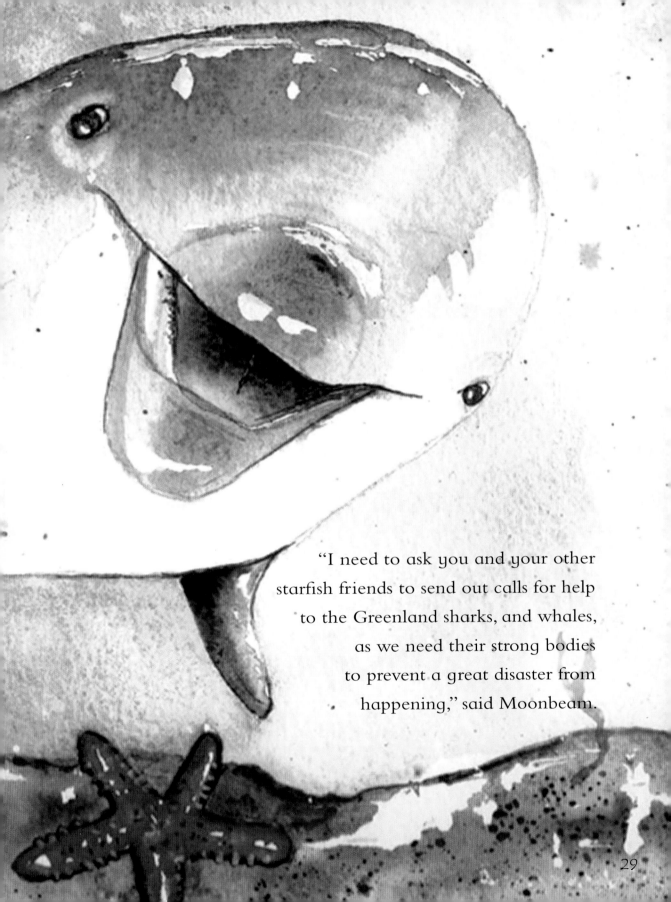

"I need to ask you and your other starfish friends to send out calls for help to the Greenland sharks, and whales, as we need their strong bodies to prevent a great disaster from happening," said Moonbeam.

Moonbeam swam out of the cave.

"Thank heavens! I thought you would never come back," said Sunbeam.

"Don't worry, Grace was so helpful. But now we must swim back up to the surface to meet the Greenland sharks who are coming to help us."

As soon as they reached the surface
they were met by a giant shark.

"Hello," said Harry with a friendly smile.

"Grace asked us to help you,
and here we are, all ready to go."

A shoal of sharks waited
patiently behind Harry.

"Do you want us to
push something?"

31

"Yes," replied Moonbeam, "but it won't be easy. There are icebergs floating south, Inuit children and polar bears are stranded on two of them. If possible, we could try and steer them towards Iceland, and safety!"

"Lead on," cried Harry. "We'll be right behind you!"

Two Inuit children crouched on one of the icebergs. Tatigat was the older brother of Panerack, his sister. Tatigat was trying to catch some fish for them to eat because they were so hungry. Panerak was worrying about their grandmother Elena at home in their village of Daneborg in Greenland.

Panerak's parents had been lost at sea during a fishing trip and now Elena would be very worried about her missing grandchildren. But just then, up popped Moonbeam and Sunbeam, with broad grins on their faces.

"Don't worry," said Moonbeam,
"we'll soon take you to a safe place."

Tears ran down Panerak's face as Tatigat dropped his fishing rod and put his arms around her.

Not far behind the Inuit children, there were three polar bears stranded on another iceberg.

"Stay close to me," said Crystal to her two baby bears, Snowdrop and Snowflake, and they immediately scurried between their mother's legs.

Crystal was a very large female polar bear and she would not put up with any nonsense from her babies OR anyone else for that matter!

Then suddenly, out of the water popped a big white head. "Hello," said Bella. "I've come to bring you some good news."

Crystal was not pleased and let out a low growl which sent surging ripples of water towards Bella.

Bella coughed and spluttered, but she wasn't frightened by Crystal, not as long as she was in the ocean, anyway!

"It's good news, not bad, please listen! A group of friendly Greenland sharks and fin whales are swimming this way and they are going to try and push you to safety towards the coast of Iceland."

Crystal lowered her head and snuggled her baby bears to her large body.

Bella thought she saw a teardrop rolling down Crystal's face.

The captain of an Icelandic coastguard ship was looking through his binoculars at the large icebergs floating southwards.

Then, he suddenly spotted the Inuit children, and the polar bears.

"Action stations!" shouted Captain Lars Gunnarsson.

"All hands on deck. We have an emergency!"

The ship's alarm siren sounded and the crew ran quickly to their posts.

As they sailed nearer to the icebergs the captain and crew saw a remarkable sight.

A great shoal of whales and sharks were pushing the icebergs towards them.

Captain Gunnarsson gave the order for the crew to lower the lifeboats, then steer them towards the icebergs and attach large safety nets and towing ropes.

Once secured, the large coastguard ship began towing the icebergs towards Reykjavik on the south-west corner of Iceland.

News had reached Reykjavik – and its harbour walls were lined with hundreds of Icelanders cheering and waving flags as the children and polar bears were brought to safety.

Moonbeam and Sunbeam were leaping in and out of the water, and the sharks and whales were swimming in circles and flapping their great tails.

Moonbeam and Sunbeam were so happy that their courage and great effort had...

# 'Made a Difference!'

Also by the author:

The Crystal Fountain

by David Morgan Williams
and illustrated by Laura Jenkins

y Lolfa

£5.99 (hb)

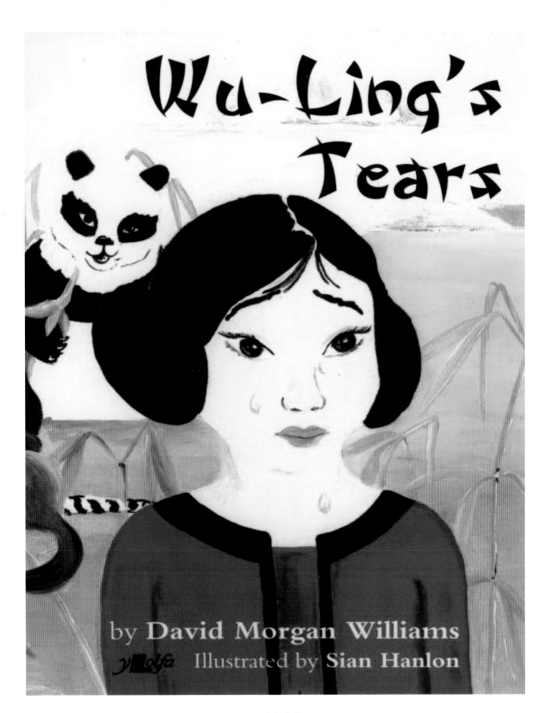

# Wu-Ling's Tears

by **David Morgan Williams**

Illustrated by **Sian Hanlon**

£3.95

*Moonbeam's Artic Adventure* is just one of a whole range of publications from Y Lolfa. For a full list of books currently in print, send now for your free copy of our new full-colour catalogue. Or simply surf into our website

## www.ylolfa.com

for secure on-line ordering.

TALYBONT CEREDIGION CYMRU SY24 5HE
*e-mail* ylolfa@ylolfa.com
*website* www.ylolfa.com
*phone* (01970) 832 304
*fax* 832 782

Printed by Y Lolfa
*Ask for a quote*